The Boxcar Children Mysteries

THE PET SHOP MYSTERY

created by
GERTRUDE CHANDLER WARNER

Illustrated by Charles Tang

SCHOLASTIC INC.
New York Toronto London Auckland Sydney

Activities by Nancy E. Krulik
Activity illustrations by Alfred Giuliani

ISBN 0-590-64804-7

12 11 10 9 8 7 6 5 4 3   1/0

Printed in the U.S.A.   4(

First Scholastic printing, October 1996

Contents

CHAPTER 1

Something to Squawk About

The Alden children pulled a wagon down the street, taking turns tossing rolled-up newspapers onto the porches and steps of each house.

"Good one," Henry, a tall fourteen-year-old, said to six-year-old Benny. "Right in front of the door, just the way Mr. Fisher likes it. I guess that's it for today."

But that wasn't it for Watch, the Aldens' dog. Something made his ears prick up. He took off for the dogwood tree on the corner.

"Watch! Watch! Where are you going?"

twelve-year-old Jessie Alden called out. She ran after her dog. "Do you see a squirrel up there?"

Henry, Violet, and Benny Alden raced over to the tree. What was making Watch so excited?

"Squirrels don't mean a thing to Watch," Henry said. "He must have seen something else."

The four children stood at the foot of the tree and stared up. All they could see were leaves and branches. But a second later, they heard a voice.

"Watch! Watch!" an odd voice squawked.

To see better, ten-year-old Violet brushed back a few wisps of her dark hair. "Somebody's up in the tree. Somebody who knows Watch."

"Watch! Watch!" the odd voice repeated.

By now Benny Alden was jumping up and down. "I see it! I see it!" he said to his brother and sisters. "It's not a somebody. It's a gray parrot."

Nearly hidden in the branches was a light

gray bird. It looked quite at home in the dogwood tree.

Watch raced around in circles. He whined and sniffed. He scratched the tree trunk. But none of that got him any closer to this talking bird who knew his name.

"Watch! Watch!" the parrot squawked again.

Jessie tapped her forehead. "Of course! That's Grayfellow from the Pretty Bird Pet Shop. Remember how the owner, Mrs. Tweedy, told us he liked to peck at shiny things like jewelry and her watch when she feeds him? I bet that's why he said 'watch' when we called Watch's name."

Watch plopped himself down on the grass. He rested his head on his paws. A silly bird had gotten the better of him.

Henry clipped a leash to Watch's collar. "Come on, boy. Let's go get Grandfather and come back with the car and a ladder. We'll give Mrs. Tweedy a call to let her know we found her missing bird. There's a bundle of old newspapers we have to give her anyway."

After Henry left, Benny got a good idea. He dug into the pocket of his jeans. "I have some sunflower. seeds. Maybe Grayfellow will come out when he sees a good snack."

Before Benny could get out his seeds, the children heard more noise. This time it was coming from the nearby bushes.

Jessie grabbed Benny's arm. "Shhh. I hope that's not a cat," she whispered. "Let's leave Grayfellow up in the tree until Henry gets back."

The children heard branches crackling. Something was moving in those bushes. Jessie tiptoed over and carefully parted the branches. "Arthur!" she screamed when she saw a boy's face stare back at her. "Why are you hiding in these bushes?"

The boy wriggled his way out and turned to leave without answering Jessie.

"Don't go," Jessie said in a gentle voice. "We didn't mean to scare you. What are you doing here?"

The pale, thin boy mumbled something the Aldens couldn't hear.

Jessie moved closer to him. "Arthur, come

meet my brother Benny and my sister, Violet. You've probably seen them around school. Violet, Benny, this is Arthur Byrd. He's in my class."

"Were you playing hide and seek?" Benny asked.

"Uh . . . no," Arthur answered. "I was looking for my cat. She's lost."

"Guess what?" Benny asked. "We found a lost animal, but not a cat. A parrot. It belongs to Mrs. Tweedy at the Pretty Bird Pet Shop. My big brother went to get a ladder. We're going to get this parrot down. Maybe we can look for your cat, too."

Arthur put his hands in his pockets, then took them out. He started to say something but stopped. Finally he spoke up. "I, uh . . . I'm going by the pet shop. I know Grayfellow, too, I'll take the parrot back. Can I?"

Jessie was puzzled. "Thanks, Arthur, but don't you want to keep looking for your cat?"

The boy bit his lip and stared down at his sneakers. "Um . . . never mind. I have to go home. I'm late." And with that, Arthur Byrd ran down the street.

Benny noticed something Arthur had left behind. He bent down and picked up a small package of sunflower seeds. "Hey, Arthur," he called after the boy, "you forgot your snack."

"That's so strange," Violet said to Jessie. "How did Arthur know it was Grayfellow in the tree? And why would he want to take him back to the pet shop instead of searching for his cat?"

Jessie looked down the street. "That *was* strange. And I wonder why he's way over on this side of Greenfield looking for his cat. He lives on the other side of town. He's so shy. If he hadn't left so fast, we could have asked him."

"Maybe Arthur can't have a real pet, so he made up a pretend pet," Benny suggested.

Jessie mussed Benny's curly hair. "You might be right about that, Benny. He's always by himself. Well, at least we found one pet. I guess we'd better see what we can do about getting Grayfellow back to the pet shop. We can do it without Henry, I guess."

Benny dug into his pocket again. "I have

sunflower seeds, too. Let's see if Grayfellow wants a snack."

As soon as the parrot saw the delicious seeds, Grayfellow stretched out his long claws. One by one, branch by branch, the African gray parrot made his way down the tree to the lowest branch.

Benny held up a handful of seeds, then whistled.

Grayfellow studied Benny, Violet, and Jessie. With a flutter of his wings, he flew onto Benny's arm. Now that Grayfellow was safe, Benny stayed as still as possible. He wanted the bird to trust him. "Here, boy. Here, boy," he whispered.

"Here, boy. Here, boy," Grayfellow said back. Then the parrot got to work on those sunflower seeds.

Like most African gray parrots, Grayfellow was a good talker. He knew about ten words, and Benny wanted to hear them all. The children took turns feeding Grayfellow. The parrot hopped onto Violet's arm and began to play with the pretty bracelet she had made the summer before.

"Now, now." Violet stroked the bird's soft gray head. "Don't unhook my bracelet. Just play with it until we take you back to Mrs. Tweedy."

"Tweedy, tweedy," the bird said.

"That's right. Mrs. Tweedy."

Grandfather chuckled when he arrived with Henry. "I told Henry we wouldn't need a ladder. I knew you three would get that bird down from the tree on your own. I wonder how he got loose in the first place. Agnes Tweedy is pretty careful with all her animals."

"On sunny days," Jessie began, "Mrs. Tweedy likes to take Grayfellow out of his cage and put him on an open perch in the store window. If that little door to the store window was left open by mistake, he could have flown out the little door, through the store, and right outside! Even with clipped wings, Grayfellow can fly . . . just not too far."

Grandfather Alden nodded. "You know, that's true. Only last week when I was picking up dog food, Grayfellow was loose in the store. He landed on my arm and started pecking at my watch."

"Watch! Watch!" the bird squawked again, and everyone laughed.

Mr. Alden drove slowly into Greenfield. He avoided every bump along the way so Grayfellow wouldn't get upset in the car.

Benny loved having a parrot in Grandfather's car. He hoped everyone in Greenfield was watching. "Know what?" he asked. "How come Grayfellow was all the way on Maple Street if he can't fly too far?"

"Hmm," Grandfather Alden said, turning up Main Street. "That's a good question, Benny."

CHAPTER 2

Feathers, Fins, and Fur

Mrs. Tweedy was at the curb as soon as Grandfather Alden's car pulled up. "Thank you so much, James, for bringing back Grayfellow. And thank you children for being clever enough to catch him."

After their grandfather left, the children gathered around Mrs. Tweedy.

Benny just had to tell her about their adventure. "A boy named Arthur was trying to find his cat. He knows Grayfellow, too. Then the boy ran away."

Mrs. Tweedy fiddled with her earring.

"Oh, I think I know who you mean. A boy named Arthur often comes in here. Such a shy boy. I always get the feeling he wants to tell me something. He only seems happy visiting my animals, especially Grayfellow. In fact, the last time Grayfellow escaped, Arthur brought him back."

"This time we brought him back, Mrs. Tweedy." Violet held out her arm for the older woman to take the parrot.

"Tweedy," Grayfellow said. The parrot pecked at Mrs. Tweedy's silver earrings.

"Naughty boy," Mrs. Tweedy scolded, but she didn't mean it. "Well, then, let's get you safely back into your cage."

The Aldens followed Mrs. Tweedy into the shop. A man the children hadn't met before stood behind the counter.

Jessie poked Henry. "That must be the new manager Mrs. Tweedy hired," she whispered to her brother. "He doesn't look very friendly. I hope he doesn't think we let Grayfellow escape."

The man stared at the Aldens.

Finally Mrs. Tweedy called him over.

"Oh, Mr. Fowler, let me introduce you to some friends of mine. They found Grayfellow while they were on their paper route. You'll be seeing the Aldens while I'm gone. They often drop off old newspapers for our bird and animal cages."

Mr. Fowler went right on feeding some goldfish. "I met one of them just a while ago, thank you."

The Aldens looked at each other, then at Mrs. Tweedy.

"But we were in school," Jessie said. "Then we did our paper route. In fact, we haven't been in this shop for a few weeks."

"Well, a boy who is always hanging around here came by earlier this afternoon, snooping and bothering our birds. Probably went poking around where he didn't belong. Next thing I knew, that parrot was gone," Mr. Fowler said, shaking far too much fish food into the aquarium. "Children shouldn't be allowed in here without an adult."

"Now, now, Mr. Fowler," Mrs. Tweedy said. "You'll get used to having children in the store once you've been here awhile. After all, it was that boy who found Grayfellow the last time he got loose. Now the Aldens have found him. Most children are wonderful with animals."

"Well, all I know is that the parrot disappeared right after I saw a boy in here, maybe even one of these kids."

Mrs. Tweedy's face grew bright pink. "May I see you out front, Mr. Fowler? Let's collect the newspapers that Mr. Alden left on the sidewalk and take them to the storage building."

Mr. Fowler put down the fish food box without replacing the lid. "I can't be carrying things outside and tending the store at the same time, Mrs. Tweedy," the children overheard him complain.

The Aldens usually loved browsing in the Pretty Bird Pet Shop, but not after hearing Mr. Fowler. Although Benny had permission from Mrs. Tweedy to pet Doughnut, the guinea pig, today he didn't feel like it. Violet even skipped her visit to her two favorite parakeets, Milo and Magic.

"No more long faces," Mrs. Tweedy said

when she returned. "Mr. Fowler is very grateful that you found Grayfellow. Truly he is. In fact, he has some notion that we should carry more unusual birds like Grayfellow. Of course, I wouldn't dream of it. The bigger birds don't belong in my small pet shop."

Violet's blue eyes widened. "You're not planning to sell Grayfellow, are you?"

Mrs. Tweedy shook her head. "Never. I promised Dr. Scott from the animal shelter that I would care for Grayfellow myself after he was abandoned. My canaries and parakeets are the biggest birds I care to sell."

Jessie stroked Grayfellow's head with the back of her finger. "Why does Mr. Fowler want to sell bigger birds?"

Mrs. Tweedy shrugged. "I don't know, really. Parrots are quite expensive, in the thousands of dollars. I suppose it would mean more money. But I have no such plans. I do hope Mr. Fowler will come around to my way of doing things. He's taking a while to get used to his job here. This is the second time Grayfellow got away."

Benny looked up at Mrs. Tweedy with his big brown eyes. "We're animal finders. We wouldn't let an animal get lost."

Mrs. Tweedy patted Benny's curly head. "Of course you wouldn't, Benny. I know how good you Aldens are with animals. Dr. Scott has often told me what a help you are at the shelter."

The children were all smiles now.

Mrs. Tweedy pushed her glasses on top of her fluffy white hair. "You know, I've been thinking of getting someone to help Mr. Fowler with some of the jobs in my shop. He might get used to the work sooner if he had a helper. Problem is, I'll be traveling for the next few weeks, and I won't have a minute to interview anyone."

Jessie lined up several cat food cans on the shelves so they were nice and straight. "Maybe Dr. Scott knows someone from the animal shelter. There are lots of volunteers."

That's when Mrs. Tweedy winked at the children. "I don't suppose you children would be available a few hours a day after school, and maybe a couple of weekends?"

"When can we start?" Henry asked.

"How about right now?" Mrs. Tweedy asked. She pulled out a clipboard from under the counter. "I made up this job list for Mr. Fowler. But I'll check off the small jobs that are just right for the four of you."

"I can clean Doughnut's cage," Benny piped up. "And make sure he and the other guinea pigs get brushed and petted every day. Isn't that what guinea pigs like?"

Mrs. Tweedy smiled. "That's just what guinea pigs like, Benny, especially when they're in a pet shop. If someone can groom them once a day, they will make much friendlier pets. I'll put you down for that job."

Benny went up to the guinea pig cage. "Can I start now?"

"Of course," Mrs. Tweedy said.

Benny found a grooming brush. He opened the cage door and gently lifted Doughnut out. Soon Doughnut was squeaking the way guinea pigs do when they are happy.

Jessie stood over Mrs. Tweedy's shoulder

to see what else needed doing. "Henry and I can make some of the deliveries or go feed pets if the owners are away. A lot of your customers know us from my paper route anyway. We can do two jobs at the same time."

"Don't you think I can do more than one job at a time, Mrs. Tweedy?" Mr. Fowler demanded when he returned and overheard Jessie.

Mrs. Tweedy waved over Mr. Fowler. "Of course you can. I was just about to tell the Aldens that. In fact, you'll be doing much more than two jobs while I'm gone. And one of them will be supervising the Aldens."

"These kids?" Mr. Fowler asked, almost shouting. "I thought I was in charge of running the shop, not looking after a bunch of kids."

Mrs. Tweedy took a deep breath before she spoke. "They need very little supervision. Before their grandfather found them, the Aldens lived on their own in a boxcar in the woods. They did very well for themselves. They are hardworking, clever children. They can clean cages and help with the feeding and deliveries. That will free up your time for the bigger jobs."

Mr. Fowler banged a box of dog food cans on the counter. "What if they let the animals loose? That's what happened today."

Mrs. Tweedy's face grew red for the second time that day. "The Aldens had nothing to do with Grayfellow getting out, Mr. Fowler. I'm sure it happened because you've had too much to do. Now you'll have more time to supervise everything. I'm counting on you for that."

This seemed to calm down Mr. Fowler a bit. "All right," he agreed. "But make sure they know exactly what jobs on that list are theirs and what ones are mine."

Mrs. Tweedy nodded. "First of all, I want you to get to know the Aldens so you don't confuse them with other children. Henry is the oldest and Jessie the next oldest. They're both strong and very organized."

Mrs. Tweedy pointed out Violet and Benny, who were already on the job. "You'll be happy to have those two around, Mr.

Fowler. Violet and Benny are so gentle with animals. They know how to give them attention without getting them nervous. Their second cousin Soo Lee is welcome here, too. Remember, you sold her a hamster a couple of weeks ago? She's been wonderful with it."

Mr. Fowler stared at the children but didn't seem to believe Mrs. Tweedy. "Don't see why the animals should be handled anyway. They're not playthings."

"Animals aren't playthings, Mr. Fowler, but they do like to play," Mrs. Tweedy said, going over to pet Doughnut. "I want all my animals to enjoy people so they'll make good pets. While I'm gone, no matter how busy everyone gets, I hope each of you — including you, Mr. Fowler — will give all my critters plenty of attention."

"We will!" the Aldens yelled, so loudly that no one noticed Mr. Fowler didn't join in.

CHAPTER 3

A Mysterious Note

On the way home, the Aldens planned their pet shop schedules. Jessie walked along the sidewalk, reading her list.

"I divided all the chores. Some have to be done every few days. But some jobs are daily — like filling water bottles and feeding the animals who need to eat every day."

"Like me?" Benny asked, stopping in the middle of the sidewalk. "I have to eat every day. And lots more than once. I wouldn't make a good turtle or fish."

Jessie gave Benny a friendly pat on the

shoulder. "You do make a good helper, though. After school we'll do our newspaper route on the way to the pet shop. As for the pet-sitting and deliveries, we can do some of those jobs at the end of the day, on our way home."

The children turned into the driveway. When they caught a whiff of something delicious, they walked a little faster — so fast that they missed seeing Arthur Byrd in the shadows. He had followed the Aldens all the way home from the Pretty Bird Pet Shop.

Watch and Mrs. McGregor, the family housekeeper, were in the kitchen when the children burst in with their news.

"We have jobs! Guess what kind?" Benny cried. He raced over to the stove to see what was cooking for dinner. "Yum! Beef stew."

He sniffed the cornbread cooling on the counter. "When's dinner?"

Mrs. McGregor sliced into the cornbread and held out a piece for Benny. "Test this to make sure it's done. We're eating at six-thirty instead of six. Your cousins Joe and Alice are coming to dinner with Soo Lee.

That's why I made cornbread to go with the beef stew your cousin Joe likes so much."

Benny smacked his lips. "And I like so much, too."

Mrs. McGregor's beef stew disappeared in no time. Joe Alden had an extra helping, and so did Benny. The only one who didn't seem to eat much was Soo Lee Alden, the little Korean girl Joe and Alice Alden had adopted.

"Don't you like beef stew?" Benny asked Soo Lee. "It's good."

"I have a surprise," Soo Lee answered, "but I can't tell."

"Shhh," Cousin Alice said to Soo Lee. "We're almost done. In a few minutes you can show Benny your surprise."

Now Benny Alden had a problem. He loved surprises, and he loved dessert. How could he sit still when he was waiting for both of them? "Can you give me a clue, Soo Lee?" he begged.

Soo Lee's brown eyes were serious. She shook her head without saying a word.

"Now, Benny, don't make it so hard for

Soo Lee," Mr. Alden said. "When you're seven years old, it's hard to keep secrets."

Henry came in from the kitchen with Jessie, just in time to keep Soo Lee from telling her surprise.

"Gingerbread, everybody!" Jessie set down a glass plate with a big square of gingerbread on the table. Henry carried in a bowl filled with whipped cream.

After the grown-ups took their servings, Benny passed the cake plate to Soo Lee. "I know Mrs. McGregor's gingerbread isn't the surprise."

Soo Lee took a tiny piece. She didn't like sweets nearly as much as Benny did. She watched Benny clean every last crumb from his plate. Finally she whispered to her mother, "Can I show Benny our surprise now?"

Cousin Alice gave Benny a huge grin. "Yes, now is the perfect time. Everybody out to the boxcar."

The three adults and five children trooped to the boxcar.

Everyone could hear Watch whining from

the house. This only made the children more excited about Soo Lee's surprise.

"Not another parrot?" Benny cried, hoping it just might be.

Soo Lee shook her head. "It's not a parrot."

"Hey, you brought your new hamster, Squeaky!" Benny cried when he saw a small animal cage on a table. "That's a good surprise, Soo Lee."

"That's not the surprise," Soo Lee said.

Cousin Joe took Benny by the hand. "Look inside."

Benny stood over the cage and looked in. "Hey, Squeaky lost weight!"

Alice and Joe couldn't keep from laughing.

"Not only did Squeaky lose weight," Alice Alden began, "but we also discovered that Squeaky isn't a he but a she. She had a litter of hamster pups two weeks ago. That's Soo Lee's surprise."

Soo Lee opened the cage door. She gently lifted a tiny golden mouselike creature out of the cage. "There were two boy hamsters and two girl hamsters. You can have this boy hamster because you're a boy, Benny."

Benny looked up at Grandfather, who had returned from quieting down Watch. "May I keep the hamster, Grandfather? It doesn't look like he eats too much."

"Hamsters make wonderful pets, Benny," Mr. Alden said. "Agnes told me what happened a few weeks ago when Mr. Fowler started working there. He mixed up the male and female hamsters. By mistake he sold Alice and Joe a female hamster that was about to have pups, instead of a male hamster."

Alice picked up the hamster pup and stroked it. "Imagine our surprise two weeks ago," she began, "when Soo Lee and I went to feed Squeaky and we found a cage full of little Squeakies! They were quite pink and bald and no bigger than my little finger."

"They grow faster than we do, Benny," Soo Lee told her cousin. "I kept the babies a secret the whole time."

Mr. Alden was smiling. "I know it's not really funny, but Agnes said several people who bought hamsters when Mr. Fowler first started working got the same surprise. Hamsters, hamsters, and more hamsters!"

Alice returned the pup to the cage. "Some people asked for their money back. But we knew just the place for one of Squeaky's pups. Some of the neighborhood children will get the others in the litter."

Soo Lee looked up at her cousins. "Mrs. Tweedy told my dad I can work at the shop, too."

"We know, we know." Violet hugged Soo Lee. "It will be so much fun taking care of the animals. We can't wait."

Cousin Joe handed Henry a bag with the words PRETTY BIRD PET SHOP on it. "You'll find hamster food and a water bottle in there, Henry."

Henry reached into the bag. "Hey, there's a mix-up, Cousin Joe. This is turtle food. And I don't see a water bottle in here, either."

Joe Alden shook his head. "Not again! Mr. Fowler took the phone order for the cage and supplies before we came over here. He's so disorganized, I bet he forgot. There will be hamster babies all over Greenfield with the way he does things. The sales slip is in the bag — unless Mr. Fowler forgot that, too. Maybe when you go to the pet shop you can exchange the turtle food."

After the grown-ups went back inside, the younger Alden children took turns playing with Benny's new hamster. They voted on names for the hamster and decided on "Pipsqueak."

Jessie was too busy thinking to play with Pipsqueak. "I can't figure out why Mrs. Tweedy hired somebody who keeps mixing up everything, including hamsters. Can you, Henry?"

Henry scratched his head. "I can't figure it out, either. Mrs. Tweedy told Grandfather that Mr. Fowler had a good recommendation from another pet shop. But he doesn't seem to care about animals enough to make sure they get the right kind of "

"Henry. Look at this sales slip!" Jessie interrupted when she started to put the receipt back in the bag. "There's a message on the back."

Henry leaned over Jessie's shoulder. " '*Delivery, five o'clock Thursday. One macaw and one woolly*' . . . I can't make out what that word is."

"Tomorrow's Thursday," Jessie said, "our first day of work. So I guess we'll find out what a woolly something-or-other is. A macaw is a parrot, the biggest kind. It's funny Mrs. Tweedy would get a delivery when she's going to be away."

"Especially a parrot," Henry said. "Didn't she just tell us she doesn't ever plan to sell any large birds, not even Grayfellow?"

Jessie folded the receipt in half. She put it in the bag with the turtle food. "I sure hope we find out what Mr. Fowler is up to tomorrow at five o'clock."

CHAPTER 4

Mix-ups and Fix-ups

The next afternoon, the Aldens zoomed through their paper route. Jessie even put Soo Lee to work so everyone could get to the Pretty Bird Pet Shop as soon as possible.

"Last one, Soo Lee," Jessie said when they reached the end of the route. "Usually we let Watch bring a paper up to this house. He likes to play with Cody, the dog who lives here. But we have to leave him home now that we're working at the pet store, so you can put the paper on the porch. Don't worry. Cody's friendly."

Soo Lee skipped up the steps to the house. The sleepy golden retriever lying on the porch thumped her tail when she saw Soo Lee.

"Good girl!" Jessie said. "We'll stop by this house again on the way home. I noticed on Mrs. Tweedy's list that Cody is supposed to get a new flea collar. You can deliver that, too."

"I like my job," Soo Lee said.

The children turned the corner onto Main Street. An elderly woman and several children stood in front of the Pretty Bird Pet Shop. Grayfellow was back on his perch in the sunny display window so people could watch him.

"Grayfellow is a good advertisement for the shop," Jessie said when she saw all the attention the parrot was getting. She pulled on the front door. It didn't budge. "What's going on? This door is stuck."

Henry gave a pull. The door didn't move.

"Can't you children read?" the elderly lady said to the Aldens. "Look at the sign on the door. It says CLOSED."

"Closed in the middle of the day?" Henry cried. "Mr. Fowler is supposed to keep the shop open when Mrs. Tweedy is away."

The old woman didn't look a bit friendly. "It's a good thing, too, keeping all these schoolchildren out of this shop for a change."

The Aldens were much too polite to tell the woman how much Mrs. Tweedy liked having children in her shop.

Henry whispered to his brother and sisters. "Let's go out back. Maybe Mr. Fowler had some chores in the storage building. He probably needed to close the shop for a few minutes. Now that we're here, we can help him out."

The children walked down a narrow passage to a small building in back of the pet shop.

"Look, there's a light on," Jessie said. She stood on tiptoe to look inside. She wasn't tall enough. She knocked at the door.

There was no answer.

"I'll give Benny a boost up to that small window," Henry suggested. Henry easily swung Benny up. "Can you see anything, Benny?"

"I see Mr. Fowler, and he sees me." Benny rapped on the window. "Can we come in, Mr. Fowler?"

Henry set Benny down on the ground and gave another good knock. "It's the Aldens," he shouted. "We came to help with the shop. If you unlock it, we can get started."

"What should we do?" Jessie asked when no one came out. She dragged over an old milk crate to stand on so she could see inside the storage building. "There are two large empty birdcages in there," she whispered. "Mr. Fowler just threw a cover over them."

At last the door opened. Mr. Fowler stepped out. "Don't you kids have homework or that paper route to finish?"

Benny smiled up at Mr. Fowler. He did not smile back. "We did our paper route. Today we start our new jobs. That's what Mrs. Tweedy said."

Mr. Fowler double-locked the storage

building. "Mrs. Tweedy doesn't know everything. That's why she hired me."

"She told Grandfather that you go bird-watching," Violet said in her gentle voice. "I like to watch birds, too."

Violet's voice seemed to quiet Mr. Fowler. "Well, as long as you're here, you might as well get started with the list Mrs. Tweedy gave you. But mind you, that's all you do. Don't go snooping where you don't belong."

Jessie tried to stay calm. "We'll just do the jobs she checked off, Mr. Fowler. And anything else you want done, too."

Mr. Fowler took out his big key ring and unlocked the front and back doors to the shop. "What I want is to manage this shop in peace. That's what I was hired for."

The Aldens didn't say another word. They got straight to work. No use bothering Mr. Fowler on their very first day.

Henry brought in some heavy pet food boxes from outside. He opened each one and counted what was inside.

"Young man!" Mr. Fowler demanded. "Why are you taking so long? Just put the cans up on those shelves and be done with it."

Henry showed Mr. Fowler a sheet of paper. "I was just checking that everything listed on this slip is in the box. Two cans are missing. Mrs. Tweedy shouldn't get charged for them. I can call the company if you want."

Henry couldn't tell if Mr. Fowler was mad at him or at the pet food company. "I make the phone calls around here, young man. You just unpack those boxes."

"Yes, sir," Henry agreed, but Mr. Fowler's remarks bothered him. Why didn't Mr. Fowler check the delivery? Didn't he want to save Mrs. Tweedy money?

The other children tried not to get upset for Henry. There was so much to do.

Violet showed Soo Lee how to fold a small stack of newspapers so they would fit the canary and parakeet cages. The girls went about their jobs quietly so the birds wouldn't get nervous.

Jessie went from cage to cage with Benny. She showed him how to refill the water bot-

tles with fresh water and fill the food dishes with just the right amount of food.

Mr. Fowler watched everything they did until he couldn't stand it anymore. "What are you taping to each cage, young lady?"

Jessie swallowed hard before she spoke. "I cut out pictures of each kind of food that the animals should get. I'm sticking the pictures on each cage so Benny won't get the food mixed up."

"If Mrs. Tweedy didn't hire a bunch of kids, we wouldn't have to worry about mix-ups," Mr. Fowler said.

The Aldens said nothing, but they couldn't help thinking. Wasn't Mr. Fowler the one who got things mixed up?

The small brass bell over the front door rang off and on for the next hour. Customers came in, but the Aldens sent them all to Mr. Fowler. They didn't want to upset him.

One of those customers was the elderly woman they had seen in front of the shop. "Who said you could comb that guinea pig, little boy?" the woman asked Benny while waited for Mr. Fowler to get off the phone.

Benny stopped combing Doughnut. His ears turned red. "It's my job," he finally said.

The old woman came over and picked up Doughnut from Benny's lap. "This is how you do it," she told Benny as she combed Doughnut.

Mr. Fowler was off the phone at last. The old woman handed the guinea pig back to Benny. "Now do it the way I showed you."

Benny sat down. Doughnut lifted his head so Benny could comb him again.

"What's the matter?" Jessie asked when she saw Benny looking gloomy and just sitting with Doughnut.

"That lady, the one we saw outside, said I didn't know how to groom Doughnut." Benny made sure the old woman couldn't hear him. "She showed me how, but it's the same way I was doing it already."

Jessie scratched the top of Doughnut's head. "Just go ahead. Mrs. Tweedy thought you did fine, and she's the boss."

The phone rang. Mr. Fowler seemed to

be busy with the elderly lady, so Jessie picked up the receiver.

Before Jessie could speak, a man started talking at the other end. "I'm on my way, Walter. So shut down the shop. I'll meet you by the storage building in back. Five o'clock sharp."

Puzzled, Jessie held the receiver before hanging up. Was this a wrong number? It couldn't be. Mr. Fowler's first name was Walter. Jessie wrote down the man's message and took it over to Mr. Fowler. "Someone just left this message for you."

Mr. Fowler snatched the note. "Who said you could answer the phone, young lady? That's not on the job list."

"I . . . uh . . . I was right by the phone, and you were busy so . . . I'm sorry," Jessie apologized. "I just wanted to help."

Mr. Fowler was really cross now. "If you want to help, get your delivery wagon loaded up. It's about time for you kids to go home anyway. Do your deliveries like you told Mrs. Tweedy, on your way home, away from this shop."

Jessie scooped up several orders from the counter and took them out to her brother. "These are the delivery orders," Jessie told Henry. "Mr. Fowler wants us to make the deliveries now."

Henry scratched his head. "What for? The store doesn't close until six. It's not even five o'clock yet."

Jessie made sure all the boxes fit nice and snug in the wagon. "Let's just do what Mr. Fowler says. He's making Violet, Benny, and Soo Lee afraid to do anything. And that old woman keeps scolding them, too."

"Oh, no," Henry said. "And this is only our first day. Let's wait until five o'clock to see if anybody shows up. I've been meaning to ask Mr. Fowler about the mysterious message on our receipt anyway."

When Jessie and Henry went into the shop again, the old woman was gone. Mr. Fowler was on the phone again. "Yes, that's right. I'm expecting them this afternoon. You can come by tomorrow after I close up the shop. Wait, never mind. Make that late Sunday after the shop closes at six. 'Bye."

Henry and Jessie looked at each other. Did Mr. Fowler's phone call have anything to do with the note? There was only one way to find out.

Henry reached under the counter. He pulled out the bag Cousin Joe had given the children. Henry cleared his throat to get Mr. Fowler's attention.

"What is it now?" Mr. Fowler snapped.

"My cousin Joe Alden gave me this receipt for a hamster cage Benny got from my cousins," Henry began. "It says there's supposed to be hamster food and a water bottle, too. But the bag only had turtle food in it."

Mr. Fowler stared at Henry an awfully long time. "What are you talking about? Are you saying I made a mistake with this order?"

Henry shifted from one foot to the other. "Well, not exactly, sir. Maybe my Cousin Joe wanted turtle food, too. But he said he ordered hamster food and a water bottle. They weren't in the bag, even though they're on the slip."

Mr. Fowler threw down his pen. "Now, how do you know this cousin of yours didn't order just turtle food? Do you think customers don't get plenty mixed up? If I had a dollar for every mistake customers make, I wouldn't need this job."

It was no use. Mr. Fowler wasn't helping at all. Henry pulled out his wallet. He reached in for some dollar bills he'd earned from his paper route customers. "Can I pick out another water bottle and the hamster food now? I'll pay for them."

Henry put the sales slip on the counter. "Oh, by the way, this note was on the back," Henry told Mr. Fowler. "I thought you might want it."

Not looking at Henry, Mr. Fowler muttered again. "Go ahead. Pick out a water bottle. And the hamster food, too. You don't have to pay. But hurry up about it. It's time to close the shop. I have paperwork to do in back."

Benny overheard this and looked up at the clock. He had just learned to tell time. "But the little hand is only near the five. Mrs. Tweedy stays open until six o'clock."

Mr. Fowler went to the front door. He

flipped over the OPEN sign so it said CLOSED. "Mrs. Tweedy isn't here now. I decide when the shop opens and closes. Now get a move on, all of you."

Henry held up the water bottle and hamster food he'd picked out. "Shouldn't you ring this up so you can keep track of what I returned and what I bought?"

Mr. Fowler kept holding the door open. "Never mind that. Out. Out. Just go."

The Aldens scooted out and heard the door bang behind them. They all turned around at the same time, only to see the shade come down over the door and the lights go out.

The Pretty Bird Pet Shop was closed for the day.

CHAPTER 5

Special Delivery

One by one, the lights went on inside the houses the Aldens passed. There was only one more delivery left.

"My stomach is growling," Benny said. "Mrs. Tweedy didn't tell us how hungry this job would make us."

"Hang on, Benny," Jessie said. She checked off all but the last order slip. "Mrs. McGregor said she'd have dinner ready for us at six-thirty. We should be done by then."

Soo Lee put her hand in Jessie's and looked

up. "Six-thirty? Is that a long time from now?"

Jessie checked her watch. "An hour or so. But you know what? I packed some cheese and crackers. Have some now so you don't get too hungry. Henry and I just have a delivery of diet cat food to drop off at this house."

"Goody!" Benny lifted Jessie's backpack from the delivery wagon. He sat down on the grass with Violet and Soo Lee.

"Jessie, why does it say BEWARE OF DOG if they have a cat?" Violet asked when she spotted a warning sign on the front lawn.

"Oh, no," Jessie answered. "That means there's an unfriendly dog. They must have a guard dog *and* a fat cat. Let's get this delivery over with quickly, Henry."

The two older children went up the porch steps and rang the doorbell. They could hear the dog through the mail slot in the door.

"Grrr. Grrr."

"I hate that low, growly sound," Henry said to Jessie. "I hope the owner puts the dog in another room."

"Brutus! Down! Quiet! Who's out there?" a man inside shouted.

Jessie's throat felt dry. She swallowed and cleared her throat. "It's your delivery from the Pretty Bird Pet Shop."

The man's voice was very loud now. He had to shout above the dog's barking and growling. "Go away. I didn't order anything."

"We have your ten-pound bag of diet cat food," Henry called out.

"There's no cat here. If you don't leave, I'll have to let Brutus out," the man inside said to the Aldens.

The door opened suddenly. Jessie and Henry stepped back, their hearts pounding. The light behind the man made it impossible to see his face. But they couldn't miss the sound of the dog's angry growling or his size. He was huge.

"We have your cat food," Jessie repeated, barely able to speak.

The man shook his head. "I don't own a cat. I don't even like cats. There's just Brutus here. He sure doesn't like cats, I can tell you that. So just go back to where you came from, you two, or I'll have Brutus chase you away."

"Sorry to bother you," Henry said. "We must have read the wrong number on the sales slip."

"Put your glasses on next time," the man said over the dog's growls, "instead of bothering people at home." With that, the man slammed the door.

"Phew." Henry raced down the path with Jessie. "I thought we were going to be that dog's dinner."

Jessie walked under the streetlight to see better. She flipped through the order slips. Finally she found the one she was looking for. "Right here. It says right here that One-twenty Maple Street gets a ten-pound bag of Diet Meow Chow."

"Well, I'm not going to argue with a mean man *and* a mean dog. Besides, I'm so hungry, I could almost eat some Meow Chow myself. We'd better ask Mr. Fowler about it. Somebody might be waiting for this order."

Jessie nodded. "We have to go back to the

pet shop anyway. We need to get a dog flea collar for Cody at Seventy-one Maple instead of the cat collar that was marked on the order slip."

"I'd rather face Brutus again than ask Mr. Fowler about these mistakes," Henry said. "But I guess he's the only one who can help us figure out these deliveries."

The younger children were chilly and tired. Henry explained that the deliveries weren't over yet. "Tell you what. No need for all of us to go back. Jessie can take you home. I'll get the deliveries straightened out."

"But we want to come," Benny said. "That's our job. Besides, I'm not hungry anymore."

Everyone laughed at Benny's remark.

"Those aren't words we hear too often from Benny," Henry said to Soo Lee. "Let's get going, then. Maybe Mr. Fowler is at the shop finishing the paperwork he talked about."

The Pretty Bird Pet Shop was dark when the Aldens returned. All they could see inside were the dim lights of the aquariums. The bird cages were covered. The small animals seemed to be curled up, asleep in their dark cages.

"Mr. Fowler is gone," Jessie said. "I guess we can't straighten out those orders after all."

Henry waved the children toward the back. "Let's check the storage building before we leave."

The Aldens didn't mean to be sneaky, but they were very quiet children. That's how they happened to hear Mr. Fowler before he heard them.

"Just in time," Mr. Fowler said to someone the children couldn't see. "I'll be done with them a couple of days from now when Mrs. Tweedy is gone again."

The children stiffened when they heard the flapping of heavy wings and a terrible squawking.

"Get her in the cage," a second man's voice said. "And hurry up about it. I didn't have time to clip her wings. She wouldn't last long in this weather if she flew away. Open the cage door."

The Aldens heard a chattering sound, then Mr. Fowler's voice. "Is that monkey tied up? The last thing I need is a monkey running all over the place. I'm telling you, these people had better be telling the truth about wanting it. This macaw parrot I can unload easy. But a monkey? Who'd buy it?"

"Yip, yip, yip," the Aldens heard coming from the storage building.

"Awk, awk, awk," the children heard when one of the men slammed the cage door shut. "Awk, awk, awk."

Jessie straightened up. "Come on, Henry. We'll find out what's going on. The rest of you stay here," she whispered. She raised her voice. "Mr. Fowler? Mr. Fowler? Are you back there?"

"Those kids again!" Jessie and Henry overheard Mr. Fowler say as he came out of the storage building. "I told you the shop was closing at five o'clock. What about your deliveries?"

Henry stepped forward to explain. "That's why we came back, Mr. Fowler. One of the slips said to deliver a cat flea collar, but the customer needs one for her dog. And another slip had the wrong address."

Jessie thought she noticed a small smile pass over Mr. Fowler's face.

"Oh, and where was that?" Mr. Fowler asked, hiding the smile now.

"Nowhere special," Henry said. He wasn't about to let Mr. Fowler know about Brutus. "All we want to do is get the right orders to the right customers."

That's when Henry nearly jumped out of his sneakers. "Hey, hey! What's this?" he asked, when he felt something heavy leap onto his shoulder.

"This is George. It's a woolly monkey," a strange man said, stepping out from the shadows. "And I'm Jack Badham . . . uh . . . I'm from the, uh . . . Tropical Animal Society. My friend Walter here is going to watch this monkey for a couple of days until we can ship him out to a zoo."

Jessie reached up to pet the nervous, chattering monkey. "Good. He doesn't belong in a pet shop. There, there, George. Don't be afraid."

The monkey had huge eyes. He didn't seem quite as frightened when he heard Jessie's voice.

"I won't hurt you." She looked at Mr. Badham. "Why don't you bring this monkey to the Greenfield Animal Shelter for now? There's more room than in this pet shop. Our friend Dr. Scott works there. She can take care of any kind of animal."

"That is none of your concern, little girl," Mr. Fowler said. "This monkey and the parrot Mr. Badham just brought here will be going to a famous zoo in a few days. They'll be treated better there than at any shelter. What do you want now anyway?"

Henry spoke up. "We just want to take care of Mrs. Tweedy's customers the way we promised her. We need a dog collar. And we have to find out who gets this diet cat food. Do you know?"

Mr. Fowler unlocked the shop, but he didn't allow Jessie or Henry inside. When he returned, he handed Henry a dog collar and a new order slip. "Here's where the col-

lar goes. Leave the cat food here. Now get a move on."

"What was all that chattering, Jessie?" Violet wanted to know. "It was too dark to see. We heard all kinds of strange sounds."

Jessie pulled the delivery wagon down Main Street. The sight of the monkey was upsetting, but she didn't want to worry the younger children. "Mr. Fowler is watching two animals for now. They're going to a zoo in a few days. At least that's what Mr. Fowler told Henry and me."

Benny pulled on Jessie's sleeve. "Was there a real live monkey like the man said?"

"Yes," Jessie answered. "A real live monkey, but a very nervous one, Benny. And a bird that we didn't get to see. It was making an awful squawk and sounded miserable."

Benny looked up at his sister. "Do you think George and the noisy bird were the mysterious delivery Mr. Fowler wrote about on that receipt?"

Jessie nodded. "Yes, I think so. But now there's another mystery. Why are those animals at the Pretty Bird Pet Shop?"

CHAPTER 6

A Hand in the Window

The Aldens had only a half day of school the following day. After dropping off their books and feeding Watch and Pipsqueak, they headed for the pet shop.

"Goody, a half day of school," Benny said when they got to Main Street. "That means a half day of playing with animals."

Henry wasn't quite as sure about that. "Don't count on it, Benny. Mr. Fowler might not need us for that long."

"Or want us for that long, either," Jessie added quietly. "But at least Mrs. Tweedy

57

will be in today before she goes off again. Maybe she'll talk to Mr. . . . Hey, look in the window of the pet shop."

"Omigosh!" Henry cried. "Someone's trying to grab Grayfellow. Can you tell who it is? All I can see is someone's arm."

As soon as Henry spoke, the arm disappeared from the small door that led to the display window.

"Let's go," Jessie said. "Maybe we can find out who that was."

Today the Pretty Bird Pet Shop was packed. The "mystery arm" could have belonged to anyone. Mr. Fowler was there. Mrs. Tweedy was in back of the store with several customers. Jessie's classmate Arthur was on his way out the door.

"That old woman is here, too," Soo Lee whispered. "I hope she doesn't yell at us again."

The shop was busier than the Aldens had ever seen it. Never before had there been a monkey in the Pretty Bird Pet Shop. Or a macaw parrot, either.

"Looks like Mr. Fowler brought the animals in from the storage building," Jessie said. "Henry and I will check on Grayfellow," Jessie told Violet, Benny, and Soo Lee. "You three can go see if you can meet the monkey and the new parrot."

When the younger children got close to the crowd, they heard Mrs. Tweedy. "No, I'm sorry. These animals are not for sale. We're just caring for them until they go to a proper home at the zoo. Now please, step back so they don't get frightened."

After the customers left, Mrs. Tweedy called the children. "Come on over, Soo Lee, Violet, Benny. Let me introduce you to George and Rainbow. George is a woolly monkey. Rainbow is a macaw. They're both from South America."

George was sitting on Mrs. Tweedy's shoulder. He gazed down at the children with his huge brown eyes. "Yip, yip," he said.

"Yip, yip," Benny said back.

Soo Lee was more interested in the new

parrot. "Rainbow looks like all the colors in my crayon box. Blue, yellow, red, green, orange, purple."

Mrs. Tweedy smiled. "Indeed, she does have the colors of a crayon box. Rainbow is quite beautiful. Imagine her flying through the rain forest. I hated to trim her wings this morning, but I had to. I was worried she'd fly far away and go searching for her real home."

Violet could see how nervous Rainbow was. The large, long-tailed bird walked back and forth in her cage. "How did Rainbow and George get here from the rain forest?" Violet wanted to know.

Mrs. Tweedy's eyes grew shiny and sad. "Mr. Fowler said they were probably brought into the country illegally and bought by someone who couldn't care for them. Whoever it was dropped them off in front of my shop last night. Poor Rainbow. Most parrots sold in shops are born and bred here. They are used to being indoors and don't mind it. But Rainbow and George came from a real forest."

"Are George and Rainbow homesick?" Soo Lee asked. "I get homesick for Korea sometimes."

Mrs. Tweedy smiled. "I think they *are* homesick, Soo Lee. They belong outdoors again. Mr. Fowler said he has made arrangements for them to go to a zoo that has a tropical area. They will be more at home there."

While Mrs. Tweedy spoke with the younger children, Henry and Jessie tried to calm down Grayfellow. "Go home. Go home," he repeated.

"I guess when he saw someone at the little door, he wanted to go out," Jessie said. "I'll fetch some seeds to quiet him down. I can't tell who opened the door, can you?"

Henry shook his head. "All I know was that the person was wearing a light-colored jacket or shirt. About half the people in the shop have something like that on, including me! Even Mrs. Tweedy does."

"Who else is wearing a light-colored top?" Henry asked Jessie when she returned with a handful of bird food.

"Mr. Fowler, Mrs. Doolittle, the old woman who told Benny how to comb Doughnut. She seems nicer now that Mrs. Tweedy is here," Jessie said. "She has on a light-colored sweater. But I don't think she'd let Grayfellow out. All she does is complain about how everybody else treats the animals."

Henry held out a large seed for Grayfellow. The parrot plucked it from Henry's hand. He cracked it open in no time at all.

"Who else is in the store?" Henry asked. "I thought I spotted that boy Arthur."

Jessie nodded. "He was in the store, but he had on a dark blue denim jacket. I tried to say hi to him, but he ran out. He's so shy."

By this time Grayfellow was up on Henry's hand. "Watch. Watch," the bird said.

Henry laughed. "No, you don't, Grayfellow. You're not going to take my watch apart."

"He does love shiny things," Jessie said. "I wonder why that is with parrots."

"He's finally settling down," Henry said

when he heard the bell on the shop door jingle. "We got here just in time. Grayfellow could have gotten out again."

Henry and Jessie headed to the bird area in the back of the shop. Violet had already filled Rainbow's water bottle and food dish.

"Come see Rainbow," Violet said in her soft voice. "She wants to go home."

"Go home! Go home!" the Aldens heard Grayfellow yell all the way from the store window in front.

Mrs. Tweedy laughed. "That's the first funny thing that's happened all day. Every night I tell Grayfellow that I have to go home. That's how he knows those words."

"Smart parrot," Benny said. "Well, I don't want to go home. I want to stay here and take care of animals."

"And so you shall," said Mrs. Tweedy. "I'm so glad you children are here. I've been upset with Mr. Fowler about Rainbow and George. I suppose he was doing a good deed, but it breaks my heart to see these beautiful wild creatures cooped up."

George let Benny scratch his head through

the cage. "It's nicer in here than in the cold storage building, isn't it, George?"

Mrs. Tweedy looked alarmed. "What do you mean? Were these animals in the unheated building?"

Henry nodded. "That's where Mr. Fowler's friend dropped them off last night. We had to come back because the orders got mixed up."

Mrs. Tweedy's jaw dropped. "That's not at all what Mr. Fowler told me. He said the animals were left in a cage in front of the store. A note said the owner couldn't take care of George and Rainbow anymore."

Benny had something to add. "That happens at the animal shelter, too. People sometimes leave their pets if they get too big."

"Or too much trouble," Violet said in a sad voice. "Maybe some people shouldn't get pets."

Mrs. Tweedy was upset now. "Certainly not pets who belong in the wild. I'm going to speak to Mr. Fowler and get to the bottom of this."

CHAPTER 7

Topsy-turvy

The Aldens went about their chores that afternoon without talking much. They shredded newspapers for the hamster and guinea pig cages. Violet sprinkled pinches of food into the fish tanks. She didn't mind when she had to spray water on the plants inside the lizard tank, even though the lizard was a little scary-looking.

"There you go, Lizzy," Violet said. "You can drink the drops of water from the plants now so you won't be thirsty."

Lizzy, the lizard, stared at Violet as if she

understood every word. Soon she was flicking her long tongue at the water drops dripping from the plants.

As they worked, the children heard Mr. Fowler and Mrs. Tweedy arguing.

"You led me to understand that Rainbow and George were abandoned, Mr. Fowler. I've now discovered that a friend of yours delivered them here," Mrs. Tweedy said in a quiet, low voice.

Mr. Fowler banged something down before he spoke. "Were those kids telling stories about me? They don't know a thing. I had them out delivering orders, and they couldn't even get that right. In all the excitement, I guess I forgot to say that my old friend Jack found the animals where he works at Bird Jungle, over in Tannersville."

Mrs. Tweedy interrupted. "Then how did they wind up in my shop?"

Mr. Fowler didn't answer right away. "Well . . . uh . . . Bird Jungle had no place for them, so Jack . . . uh, came here. He remembered that I knew all about wild animals from when I worked on a fishing boat

out of South America. He couldn't leave them out on the street. He knew this was a good place."

"The rain forest was a better place," Mrs. Tweedy said in a sad voice. "Now do you understand why I don't sell animals like George and Rainbow? If no one would sell them, no one could buy these beautiful creatures. They wouldn't be taken from their homes. Now, when did you say the Tropical Animal Society will be coming for them?"

Mr. Fowler cleared his throat. "Um . . . this weekend. But before they do, why not consider selling animals and birds like that to your customers? Look how many people asked about buying them today."

Henry peeked over the shelves. Mrs. Tweedy's blue eyes were as dark as slate. "I have told you before, and this is the last time I will repeat it. The Pretty Bird Pet Shop will *never* sell wild animals or birds. Never. I'll trust you to make sure they are safely gone to the zoo by next week," Mrs. Tweedy said. "I have to go home now to pack for the convention. Are we agreed?"

"Agreed," Mr. Fowler answered, ripping open a cardboard box with his hands instead of cutting off the top with scissors.

Mrs. Tweedy called the children to the bird room. Her voice was calm again now. "I'm off for a few days, children. I've been meaning to show you something you'll enjoy doing while I'm gone. I'm going to teach you how to train young parakeets to come out onto your finger."

Violet followed Mrs. Tweedy's directions. "Just put your index finger in front of the bird over and over. Each time say, 'Hop up. Hop up.' Soon the bird will think your finger is a safe perch."

Violet held her finger very still in front of Milo. "Hop up. Hop up," she said. "It tickles," she said softly when Milo hopped onto her finger.

"What if the parakeets fly around?" Jessie wanted to know. "How would we catch them?"

"One way is to take a small lightweight cloth, like a handkerchief. I keep a few right here on this shelf. Toss the cloth gently but quickly over the bird, then pick it up. It's a very safe way to catch the bird. Then I always give them a treat when I return them to their cages."

Jessie showed Mrs. Tweedy her checklist of jobs the children had finished. "This is how I organized everything. We'll be doing the pet care jobs for Mr. Fowler on Sunday, since that's his day off."

Mrs. Tweedy nodded. "Wonderful. Now, when you go to Jerry's Gas Station to feed their two guard dogs, don't be frightened. Buster and Beau sound more dangerous than they are. Jerry built a special dog run for them in back that connects to the station. There's a hatch door where you can leave their food. Buster and Beau are used to this. There's no need for you to go in at all."

"Do Buster and Beau bite people?" Soo Lee asked Mrs. Tweedy.

"Not unless someone is trying to get into the gas station who shouldn't be there," Mrs. Tweedy said. "Anyway, the dogs are always in the dog run. Not to worry."

"We won't," Jessie said. "The only thing

I am worried about is how to get supplies. Your shop is closed on Sundays."

Mrs. Tweedy patted Jessie's hand. "No problem. Here's an extra key to the back door. Come in for anything you need. Make sure to leave the shade down on the front door so no one thinks the shop is open."

"Sure thing, Mrs. Tweedy," Henry said. "Is there anything extra you want us to do?"

"See if you can get Mr. Fowler to smile," Mrs. Tweedy whispered. "I wish he enjoyed his job as much as you children enjoy yours. He's on the grumpy side. Maybe you can cheer him up."

"We're good at cheering up animals," Benny said after Mrs. Tweedy left. "Milo and Magic like us, and so do Lizzie and Doughnut. Even Rainbow and George like us better than Mr. Fowler does."

This was true. Already the big macaw and the little monkey seemed to enjoy having the children around. Benny and Soo Lee played monkey games with George. When they tilted their heads, George tilted his. When Soo Lee hid some food in the palm of one hand, George tried to guess which hand had a treat for him.

"He's pretty smart," Benny said to Soo Lee.

"So is Rainbow. Listen," Violet said.

"Food, food," Rainbow said when Violet came around to fill up the seed dish. "She's already learned to say 'food.' "

"Too bad they have to leave," Violet said. "This might be the last time we see them before they go to the zoo."

The children spent extra time with George and Rainbow. The smaller birds in the bird room seem excited, too. The whole bird room was filled with twittering, chattering, whistling bird talk and bird song. That is until the back door banged and everybody jumped.

"Let's close the door," Jessie said. "Drafts are bad for these birds and for George. Mr. Fowler is in the storage building, so I'd better see what this customer wants."

When Jessie came out, she saw a tall, thin woman holding a small, brand-new pet carrier.

"Where is Mrs. Tweedy?" the woman demanded. "I have to see her. I specifically said the carrier I needed was for Bootsie. Why, everyone in Greenfield knows Bootsie won the Largest Cat Award in the pet show last year. This carrier wouldn't fit a mouse!"

Jessie ran over to help the customer. "Mrs. Tweedy just left. Are you Mrs. Garfield? My brother and I dropped off that cat carrier yesterday. Is it the wrong size?"

The woman's voice shook with anger. "Is it the wrong size, young lady? If you saw my Bootsie, you wouldn't have to ask that question. Bootsie couldn't get a paw into this tiny thing, let alone the rest of her."

Jessie took the pet carrier from the woman. "I'm sorry. There's my brother. Henry, can you pick out a large pet carrier for this customer? Do you have the sales slip, Mrs. Garfield?"

The woman reached into her pocket. "See, I ordered the Model Ten-eighty, but somebody crossed it out and wrote down Model Ten-twenty instead. I had to drive all the way to the vet's with Bootsie jumping around inside my car." The woman put her hand on her chest to calm herself down. "I could have had an accident! Then, to make matters worse, Bootsie ran from the car and was nearly eaten by a dog coming out of the vet's. All because of a foolish mistake."

By this time, Henry had pulled down the largest pet carrier in the shop. He handed it to the woman to calm her down. "Here, take this one. I can help you get your cat inside it if you want."

"Hmmm. I might ask you to do just that," she told Henry. "Getting Bootsie into a cat carrier is no easy task. One other thing. I never did get my monthly order of diet cat food. Could you put a bag in the car for me? Or rather for Bootsie. *I'm* certainly not on a diet."

Henry and Jessie hoped the woman would laugh, and she did. But the children couldn't help wondering. How did Mrs. Garfield's orders get switched? And why?

CHAPTER 8

A Scary Chase

Sundays were big breakfast days at the Aldens. The smell of bacon, sausage, and scrambled eggs filled the kitchen. The children sat with their grandfather and talked about their new jobs.

"Today's Mr. Fowler's day off. We get to do his pet-sitting jobs," Benny said between gulps of orange juice. "But know what?"

"What, Benny?" Mr. Alden asked.

"We have to feed Buster and Beau while they guard Jerry's Gas Station," Benny said. "And know what else? There's a little door

where we have to put the food. We don't want the dogs to think we're burglars and chase us by mistake."

Mr. Alden put down his coffee cup. "That sounds like an important job, Benny."

On Sundays it was Henry's turn to clear the table. "Mrs. Tweedy told us the dogs are kept in a dog run," he explained to his grandfather. "We won't be getting close to them. Still, we can't bring Watch along. Buster and Beau might get too excited."

Mr. Alden sat back and poured himself another cup of coffee. "I'll get Watch out for a walk in the woods this afternoon. He misses going out with you children now that you're so busy at the pet shop."

Jessie scratched Watch behind his ears. "Good boy. We'll be back early."

"Greenfield is so sleepy on Sundays," Violet said after the Aldens picked up Soo Lee on their way to town. "Hardly anyone is out."

"I'm not sleepy," Soo Lee said. "I can't wait to see the talking birds."

The children arrived at the Pretty Bird Pet Shop to pick up supplies. As soon as Henry unlocked the back door, the chattering, yipping, squawking, and twittering started up, just like an animal chorus.

"Tweedy, Tweedy, Tweedy," Grayfellow squawked from his cage.

"We're not Mrs. Tweedy," Violet said, laughing.

"Tweedy, Tweedy, Tweedy," Grayfellow repeated.

Violet stopped by the parrot's cage. "I guess he thinks anyone who comes in here is Mrs. Tweedy. I'm Violet."

Grayfellow tried to peck at Violet's bracelet right through the bars of his cage. He couldn't say "Violet" yet.

Violet, Benny, and Soo Lee went around the shop to make sure all the animals had enough water and food. When Violet stopped by George's cage, the little monkey reached out.

Violet handed him a piece of fruit. "Here's some banana from my breakfast, George. I'll miss you."

"Yip, yip," George said back.

" 'Bye, Rainbow," Soo Lee whispered to the macaw. "Do you think today is the day Rainbow and George have to go to the zoo, Jessie?"

Jessie filled a box with supplies. "Mr. Fowler said it might be this weekend. But maybe not, since he's off today. In a way, I wish George and Rainbow could stay here, even though they'll be happier in the zoo."

Henry waved everyone toward the back door. "Time to go. Let's lock up tight." He looked over the delivery list. "Our first stop is on Magnolia Street. There's a cat named Kit Kat that we have to feed. I've got the house keys Mrs. Tweedy left us."

A few minutes later, the Aldens stood in front of a small white house. "This is where Kit Kat lives," Jessie said. "The job sheet says that we should bring in the newspaper, check the mail, take in any garbage cans, and, of course, feed Kit Kat."

"Can you and Violet and I feed her?" Soo Lee asked Jessie.

"That's just what I was thinking," Jessie

said. "Here's a new box of cat food, a cat treat, too."

While Henry and Benny checked the outside of the house, the three girls let themselves in. Right away, a plump white-and-orange cat rubbed against the girls' legs and purred like a little motor.

Jessie laughed. "I guess we don't have to worry about Kit Kat being afraid of us, do we?"

Kit Kat got all excited when she heard Violet tear the wrapping off the cat food box. She purred so loudly that the girls expected her to start talking any minute.

"Cats are easy," Jessie told Henry and Benny after the girls had fed Kit Kat. "Kit Kat practically ate out of Soo Lee's hands."

The Aldens headed for Jerry's Gas Station next. This was a favorite stop whenever Grandfather Alden had to get gas. The children liked to get peanuts from the machine inside while they watched Jerry work on cars. But Sunday was Jerry's day off.

Only Buster and Beau were on duty. As soon as the two dogs heard the Aldens, they

began to snarl and bark in the most awful
way. The younger children stayed close to
Henry and Jessie.

"Not to worry," Henry said. "They're
locked up in their run."

Violet, Benny, and Soo Lee wanted to believe what Henry said. Still, that barking
sounded awfully loud!

Jessie took Soo Lee and Benny by the
hands. "Since Buster and Beau are guard
dogs, they are trained to growl."

Violet tiptoed behind the others. "They
sound so close, Jessie. Are you sure they're
always, always kept inside?"

"Of course they are, Violet. Don't be — "
but Jessie's comforting words were interrupted by Henry yelling.

"Run, Jessie! Run! Go back to the front
with the others. The dogs are loose!"

Jessie hurried the children down the alleyway. She turned around to make sure Henry
was all right. He was running right behind
them and made it through the gate, locking
it behind him.

"Grrrrr. Grrrr," the dogs growled from the other side of the gate.

"Here, Henry, I brought some treats. Maybe the dogs will eat them if we toss them over the fence," said Jessie.

Henry threw them into the dogs' pen, which was just over the fence. The dogs ran excitedly into their pen and lay down to eat their snack. Then Henry went back through the gate, quietly, and shut the dogs into their pen.

"That was close," he said aloud. He called down to the other children. "All clear. Bring the water and dog food over here."

Jessie and Violet led Soo Lee and Benny by the hands.

"Henry says it's okay to feed the dogs now," Jessie said.

Henry was right. All Buster and Beau wanted to do was eat lunch, not the Aldens! Their tails wagged at the sight of the dog food bag Violet was carrying.

"Benny, lift the small door here," Henry said. "I'll get their bowls out. Benny can pour in the dog food. And, Violet, you can fill the water bowls. They're not growling anymore."

"Is this enough water?" Violet asked after she finished pouring water from a big jug.

Henry pushed the bowls into the small opening to the dog pen. "Just right," Henry said. "Everybody did great, just great. And thanks for thinking of the dog treats, Jessie."

Jessie began to laugh. "Guess what, Henry? Those weren't dog treats. They were cat treats! I brought them along so Kit Kat wouldn't be afraid of us!"

Henry smiled. "Well, anyway, it worked. Buster and Beau are safe inside. They won't be able to get loose again unless somebody lets them out on purpose.

"Again," he added softly so the younger children wouldn't hear him.

CHAPTER 9

Little Footprints

Main Street was busier in the afternoon when the Aldens returned to the Pretty Bird Pet Shop. The children stood at the traffic light in the middle of town and waited for the light to change.

"Can I cross now?" Benny asked as soon as the light turned yellow.

"Wait, Benny!" Jessie cried, grabbing his arm. "That van is running the yellow light."

The children jumped back when a gray van whizzed past.

"Hey!" Henry cried. "Isn't that Mr. Fowler driving the delivery van from the pet shop?"

Jessie looked both ways. She wanted to make sure no more flying vans were coming. "Today's the day Mr. Fowler said Rainbow and George might be going to the zoo. But I thought the people from the Tropical Animal Society were going to pick them up, not Mr. Fowler."

Henry and Jessie guided the younger children across the street. "There's only one way to find out," Henry said. "Let's see if the van is at the pet shop or not."

Sure enough, when the Aldens got to the parking lot in back of the Pretty Bird Pet Shop, the gray delivery van was gone.

"I thought Mr. Fowler wasn't working today," Jessie said.

Benny and Soo Lee ran ahead. Were George and Rainbow really gone?

Benny leaned on the door and got a big surprise. "Whoa," he said when the door gave way and he nearly fell down. "The door wasn't closed all the way."

Jessie raced over. "Wait a minute. I

checked this door over and over. I double-locked it with Mrs. Tweedy's key."

Henry pushed past Jessie. "Let's check around, just the two of us, to see if the store was broken into. Then we can call the police."

Jessie looked down at the lock. "The store wasn't broken into, Henry. There's Mr. Fowler's key ring with the store key right in the lock. He must have gone out in such a rush, he forgot to lock up."

The children tiptoed inside. What were they going to find? Again, the twittering of dozens of birds greeted them.

Jessie grabbed Henry by the arm. "Wait, doesn't it sound different in here? Bird noises are coming from every direction."

Henry reached for the light and flipped on the switch. There was a huge flutter. Birds were flying all over the store!

"Oh, no!" Jessie cried. "Somebody let the birds out of their cages. They're everywhere. Quick, let's catch the ones we can."

Parakeets clung to shelves with their tiny claws. Some were near the ceiling where it

was warmer. Others flew back and forth from the front of the store to the back, diving and swooping nervously.

Violet was worried. "They're all confused. Let's get Mrs. Tweedy's handkerchiefs. We have to catch some of them before they hurt themselves bumping into things."

"Good idea," Henry said.

Each of the children grabbed a cloth to toss over the birds so they could catch them one by one.

"There!" Henry said when he caught his third parakeet under a handkerchief.

Violet floated a purple bandanna over a bright yellow parakeet. "We only caught a few birds, Jessie. Do you think any of them flew outside?"

Before Jessie could answer, the girls heard Benny yell from the front of the store. "Come here, everybody! Wait till you see!"

Everybody ran. What a surprise when they got to the front of the store! A flock of canaries and parakeets was crowded on the floor gobbling up birdseed.

Henry gave Benny a pat on the head.

"Smart boy, Benny. You used birdseed to get all the missing birds together."

"But, but — " Benny began.

Jessie interrupted. "Thanks, Benny. It's a lot easier to catch them this way. They are too busy eating to fly away."

"But, but — " Benny still couldn't get a word in.

"Whoa, Benny," Henry said. "Looks like you got carried away with your good idea." Henry looked up and down the aisle. Boxes of bird, fish, and turtle food were half opened. Food was spilled on the floor, on shelves, and on counters.

"Why did you throw down so much food to catch the birds — even fish food?" Henry asked.

"That's what I was trying to tell you! I didn't spill the food — it was spilled already. The birds found it by themselves," Benny said excitedly.

"I know you wouldn't spill a thing if you could help it, Benny," Jessie said. "We just thought you had a smart idea. In a way, whoever spilled this at least helped keep the birds in the store. With the door open, they might have escaped. Let's get the rest of them into their cages."

The Aldens had no trouble rounding up the birds into their cages.

"There," Henry said when all the birds were safe and sound in the bird room. "Twenty-two parakeets and eight canaries and . . . Oh, no, wait. Look who's missing."

"Rainbow!" Benny shouted.

"George!" Violet said.

They searched up and down every aisle. They checked under every counter. They didn't spy the macaw's rainbow-colored feathers anywhere or hear George's little yips, either.

"I guess they weren't interested in bird-seed. I'll go outside and look around," Henry told the others. "They might be in the stor-age building."

Violet was worried. "I hope they're not outside. It's so chilly."

Henry patted Violet's cheek. "We'll find Rainbow and George. Maybe Mr. Fowler was driving them to the Tropical Animal Society. We'll keep looking, and we'll make a few phone calls," he added before heading out the door.

Jessie pulled out the phone book. "Let's see. Nothing under Tropical Animal Society. I guess it's not close to Greenfield. I'll call Mr. Fowler. Maybe he's home by now."

Before Jessie could dial the number, the phone rang.

"Who could be calling?" Violet asked. "Nobody knows we're here."

Jessie picked up the receiver. "Yes, this is the Pretty Bird Pet Shop." She paused. "Yes! Yes, we are missing a parrot from the shop. A rainbow-colored macaw. Is she all right? I'll send someone right away. Just keep her safe so she doesn't get away again. Oh, thank you. Thank you."

Jessie turned to the other children. She was smiling from ear to ear. "Guess what? The volunteer fire department has Rainbow! Mrs. Doolittle, that elderly lady who comes in here, spotted her in a tree and called the fire department." Jessie stopped to catch her breath. "The firehouse is right nearby. So they got a ladder and some fruit and got her to come down."

By this time Henry had returned and over-heard everything. "That solves half of our problem. I'll go over to the firehouse with the big cage and bring her back."

Benny handed Henry his new baseball jacket. "Here's my jacket."

Henry made a funny face. "What for? I'm not cold. And it sure wouldn't fit me."

Benny made a funny face back at Henry. "It's not for you, Henry. It's to put over the cage to keep Rainbow warm."

"Good idea," Henry said on his way out the door. "See you later."

"We'll stay here and clean up," Jessie told her brother.

The four children knew where to find the brooms, dustpan, and a wastebasket. There was an awfully big mess to clean up.

Soo Lee bent down with a dustpan and waited for Violet to sweep the spilled fish food into it. "Look at these teeny footprints, Violet," she exclaimed. "They go all over the fish food."

The other children came over to see what Soo Lee was talking about. Sure enough, footprints, sometimes two, sometimes four, trailed through the powdery fish food.

Now Jessie looked alarmed.

"What's the matter?" Violet asked her sister.

"I think these footprints belong to George," Jessie answered. "But George isn't here. And now that we know Rainbow wasn't with Mr. Fowler, that must mean George escaped, too."

Jessie was on the phone right away. "I'm sorry to bother you about another animal," she said when she got through to the firehouse. "Could you watch out for a lost monkey? His name is George. He belongs to the Pretty Bird Pet Shop, too." Jessie paused. "Thank you. Yes, I'll be here."

"Rainbow!" Violet called out when Henry returned.

Henry removed Benny's jacket covering the large cage. "Here she is. I'm afraid she's a little nervous with all the excitement. She dropped some feathers."

Violet opened the cage door to offer a sunflower seed to Rainbow, but the bird refused it. "She's not hungry," Violet said quietly. She gathered up several pretty feathers and gave one to Soo Lee and one to Benny. "Keep these so we'll always remember Rainbow. I hope she goes to the zoo soon. She looks so sad."

Henry carried the cage to the bird room. "She'll get nice and warm in here." He helped everyone straighten out the store. "We'll have everything shipshape for tomorrow when Mr. Fowler comes in. I want to ask him about Rainbow and George and why the store door was open this afternoon."

"What about Buster and Beau?" Jessie demanded. "Tomorrow we have a lot of things to talk about with Mr. Fowler."

"Fowler. Fowler," Grayfellow said. "Fowler, Mr. Fowler."

CHAPTER 10

Monkey in the Middle

George was still missing the next day. The Aldens were under orders from Mr. Fowler. They were not to return to the Pretty Bird Pet Shop until the monkey was found.

The Aldens asked every one of their newspaper customers about George. No one had seen him. They checked every yard they passed. But still, no George.

Jessie began to roll up a newspaper to deliver. Something caught her attention on the front page. "Look at this!" She read an article out loud:

Monkey Missing

A Woolly South American monkey named George escaped from the Pretty Bird Pet Shop over the weekend. Mr. Walter Fowler, manager of the Pretty Bird Pet Shop, believes the monkey and a South American macaw both escaped when young employees of the shop left the store unlocked Sunday morning. The macaw was later recovered by the fire department. The monkey is still missing. Anyone with information about the lost monkey should call the Pretty Bird Pet Shop.

"Oh, no," Jessie said. "We didn't leave the shop unlocked. Mr. Fowler did. Why won't he give us a chance to explain how we found the keys and everything?"

Henry put his arm around Jessie's shoulder. "He's probably afraid Mrs. Tweedy will fire him if he admits his mistake."

"If only he'd listen," Jessie said. She kicked

some leaves along the sidewalk on the way to Main Street.

When the Aldens reached the corner, Mrs. Doolittle spotted the children before they saw her. She marched over. Her shopping bag swung from one arm and her black umbrella from the other. "I understand you lost Mrs. Tweedy's new animals!" she said before the Aldens could even say hello. "I told Mrs. Tweedy and Mr. Fowler the same thing. If they needed extra help in the shop, they should look for a responsible adult."

Benny tried to hold back what he had to say, but he couldn't. "We didn't lose George and Rainbow. Somebody forgot to lock the door."

Mrs. Doolittle looked at Benny over the tops of her glasses. "Indeed! I'll have you know I went by the shop yesterday afternoon and looked through the front window. I saw you making a mess in there."

Why was Mrs. Doolittle always so upset with the Aldens?

"We were cleaning up," Soo Lee explained

in her squeaky voice. "We didn't spill the food."

"Nonsense!" Mrs. Doolittle said. "I was in the shop Saturday night. Everything was quite tidy until you children arrived yesterday."

The children were confused.

"When were you in the shop Saturday night?" Henry asked. "We were there until it closed. We didn't see you."

Mrs. Doolittle banged the tip of her umbrella on the sidewalk. "I'll have you know that Agnes Tweedy gave me an extra set of keys. In fact, since Mr. Fowler lost his set, it was a good thing I had them so he could open up the shop this morning."

Jessie took a deep breath before saying anything. "We found some keys that were left in the lock sometime Sunday. Maybe that's how Rainbow and George got out."

Mrs. Doolittle's mind was made up. She picked up the newspaper in the wagon. "That's not what this newspaper says. Rainbow got loose because children shouldn't be allowed to do the work of adults." With that,

Mrs. Doolittle put her umbrella under her arm and disappeared down the street.

"Should we still go the pet shop now?" Violet asked Jessie. "Mrs. Doolittle and Mr. Fowler seem like friends. They don't want us around."

Benny thought of something. "What if Mrs. Doolittle let out George and Rainbow?"

The children looked at each other.

"Hey, Benny, maybe you have something there," Henry began. "We know Mrs. Doolittle had keys. And who found Rainbow anyway? She did. Maybe she knew where Rainbow was the whole time."

Jessie was frowning. "But why would she let out the animals? She's always complaining that nobody knows how to take care of them except grown-ups. That doesn't make any sense."

The Aldens thought about this the rest of the way to the pet shop. When they arrived, Grayfellow was on his perch in the front window. Mr. Fowler was feeding him. The minute Mr. Fowler saw the Aldens, he dropped the bag of birdseed, went over to the front door, and put up the CLOSED sign.

"He shut us out," Violet said, annoyed. "I want to see Rainbow."

Henry tried to calm Violet. "Rainbow might not even be in the store anymore. I know how much you want to see her. I hope she's gone to the zoo like Mr. Fowler said. She looked pretty sick after we brought her back."

A truck from the pet food company pulled up. Mr. Peterson, the driver, recognized the Aldens. "Hey, my lucky day. Five pairs of hands to help me carry in some boxes. What do you say?"

"Sure thing, Mr. Peterson," Henry answered. "Show us what to bring in."

As the Aldens loaded up packages, Jessie whispered to everyone, "Good thinking, Henry. We'll just follow Mr. Peterson. Now Mr. Fowler has to let us in."

Sure enough, as soon as he spotted the delivery man, Mr. Fowler unlocked the front door. "Come on in," he said. "I put up the CLOSED sign when I saw some pesky customers outside. I had to catch up on some paperwork. Now that you're here, we can go over next month's orders."

Mr. Peterson carried several large boxes to the counter. "It was my lucky day. The Aldens were outside, so they're helping me with my delivery."

Before Mr. Fowler could say a thing, all five Aldens trooped into the store.

"Hey!" Mr. Fowler yelled. "What are you kids doing? Just leave the boxes on the floor. I'll put them away."

Mr. Peterson looked confused. "Gee, Walt, it's not every day you have five helpers who know what they're doing. That gives us both plenty of time to go over next month's orders. The Aldens know where everything goes."

"No, they don't," Mr. Fowler said. "They don't know where the monkey went after they left my shop wide open yesterday."

Mr. Peterson was caught in the middle. "Tell you what. I'll keep an eye out for George on my route. I guess I'd better be on my way."

After Mr. Peterson left, Henry brought

over a stack of packing slips from the shipments. "We're all done, Mr. Fowler, except for one thing." Henry reached into his jacket pocket. "Here are the store keys."

Mr. Fowler's eyes flashed with anger. "You took these keys *and* left the store unlocked?"

Henry looked Mr. Fowler straight in the eye. "No, we didn't take these keys. We found them. We saw you driving away just a couple of minutes before we got here on Sunday. Somebody forgot to lock up and left these keys in the lock."

The phone rang before Mr. Fowler had time to think of an excuse. "Out of here! All of you, out of here!" he shouted, picking up the phone.

The Aldens filed out of the store. They had just left when Jessie remembered something. "My backpack's inside. Wait here. I'll be right out."

Mr. Fowler was yelling on the phone and didn't see Jessie.

"Can I help it?" Mr. Fowler asked someone. "Look, you said they wanted the animals right away. Then what happens? They changed their minds when I got there. And what am I supposed to do with a monkey after all the trouble we went through to ship it up from South America? Anyway, I brought back the animals. Then, wouldn't you know that monkey made a mess of things, dumping boxes and opening cages? I guess he went wild."

Jessie couldn't hear the person on the other end of the phone, but Mr. Fowler wasn't finished. "The monkey will turn up. Just give me until Saturday," Mr. Fowler said. "Only this time, make sure whoever you line up really wants the animals. See you Saturday night. Yeah, I'll have both of them by then if I have to search day and night."

Jessie bent down to grab her backpack. She tried not to make too much noise. Could she get out of the store without Mr. Fowler seeing her? What was he planning for Saturday night?

CHAPTER 11

Monkey See, Monkey Do

The Aldens searched Greenfield day and night for George. Now that Mr. Fowler didn't want them in the shop they had a lot more free time. They put up notices around town. Even Grandfather Alden tried to help. Whenever his grandchildren got a call that the monkey had been sighted, he drove the children around to search for him. But when Saturday arrived, George was still on the loose.

"I guess we should go home now," Henry said after a long car search on Saturday morning. "George seems to get away just before we arrive. It's so frustrating."

"He's afraid of people," Violet said. "That's why he doesn't stay in one place."

Jessie stared at every bush and tree they passed. "I just want to make sure we find George before Mr. Fowler does. I know he's got something planned for tonight."

Violet gazed out the car window, too. George was somewhere out there. They just had to find him.

Grandfather Alden turned into the driveway of his house. "I doubt Mr. Fowler will have any more luck than we have with George. After all, he's in the shop all day."

When the Aldens got home, Mrs. McGregor was at the door. "Don't take your jackets off. Just get over to Seventy-three Oak Street right away. A woman there found George in her garage. He was sound asleep in her car! Can you imagine? She saw your notice on the supermarket bulletin board and called here."

"It's okay, Grandfather," Henry said when Mr. Alden put his hat back on. "You don't have to drive us. Oak Street is only a couple of streets over. We'll take our bikes — and Watch — this time. That way we can spread out in case George gets away again. And Watch will be a big help. When we have George for sure, we'll call you to bring the car."

Watch barked twice as if he understood exactly what Henry had said. The children were on their bikes in no time. Watch followed along the sidewalk, staying right near everyone.

"Stop sign," Jessie reminded Benny and Violet when they got to the corner of Oak Street. "We take a right turn here. It's just a few houses down."

At that very moment, a van screeched up to the other stop sign, then raced through.

"Oh, no," Jessie cried. "It's Mr. Fowler! I hope he's not coming from the house where George was found. Let's get there, quick!"

When the children arrived at the house, they jumped off their bikes and went straight to the garage. Watch sniffed around everywhere.

"Where is he, Watch?" Jessie asked. "Do you see George?"

Watch sniffed all the way down the driveway, then stopped.

"George is gone, isn't he, Watch?" Jessie asked.

A young woman came out to the garage to find out what was going on.

Henry introduced everyone. "Hi, we're the Aldens. Sorry we went into your garage. We got your call about the missing monkey and came straight over."

The woman seemed confused. "But he's not missing anymore. The manager from the Pretty Bird Pet Shop just picked him up."

"Oh, no!" Jessie cried. "That was Mr. Fowler. He said he's sending him to a zoo, but we're not sure. How did Mr. Fowler find out George was here? We came as fast as we could."

"After I left a message at your house, I called my neighbor over. My neighbor remembered a newspaper article that said the monkey was missing from the Pretty Bird Pet Shop, so I called there next. Wasn't that the right thing to do?" the woman asked.

Jessie didn't want the woman to feel bad. "It's okay. As long as George is safe, I guess he'll be fine. Thank you for calling us."

The children said good-bye to the woman, when a surprise visitor appeared on the front lawn.

"Arthur!" Jessie said when she saw her classmate standing by the bicycles. "What are you doing here?"

Arthur was out of breath from bicycling. "Can you come to the pet shop with me? It's important. Mr. Fowler chased me away. I heard him tell somebody to meet him in the storage building. He told the person he knew where the monkey was. Then he closed the shop and left. I didn't know what to do, so I called your house. Your grandfather said you would be here. We have to go. And fast."

"Good job, Arthur," Henry said. "Let's get over there quick."

The children didn't take long to get to the pet shop. The CLOSED sign still hung on the front door.

"Let's see if anyone shows up in the parking lot," Jessie said. "We'll hide behind the Dumpster in back. We can keep an eye on the storage building from there."

The children rolled their bikes down the alleyway. They huddled behind the Dumpster.

"There's a light on in the storage building," Jessie whispered. "The milk crate is still under the window. I'll see what Mr. Fowler is up to."

Standing on her tiptoes, Jessie peeked through the window. She could see Mr. Fowler walking back and forth and checking his watch. George huddled behind the bars of a small cage. Rainbow was perched in another cage.

"Poor things," Jessie whispered when she returned. "George and Rainbow look so miserable. Shhh, there's a car coming."

The children heard a car door slam. A woman's high heels clicked along the pavement. There was a knock at the door.

"It's Mrs. Ransome," a woman called out. "I came for the animals Mr. Badham told me about."

The Aldens saw a streak of light spread across the alleyway when Mr. Fowler opened the door.

"The animals are in here," he told the woman.

"In this drafty old building?" the woman wanted to know. "Mr. Badham said they would be in the pet shop. I've always heard this shop had lovely, healthy animals. I wouldn't buy anything less for my grand-children."

"He *is* going to sell Rainbow and George!" Violet said in alarm. "They're not going to a zoo."

"These are healthy animals," Mr. Fowler said. "They're out here because I just got these new cages. Now we'd better complete the sale. The owner is due back from a trip in a while. I told her everything was all set with George and Rainbow."

"Why, this can't be the macaw Mr. Badham told me about!" the woman interrupted. "What's the matter with this bird? It has so little color. I'm sure you don't mean this is the bird Mr. Badham arranged for me to buy for my grandchildren. This won't do at all."

The Aldens heard Mr. Fowler clear his throat a few times. What was he going to say next? "Well, it's, uh . . . the shedding season."

Benny poked Jessie with his elbow. "That's not true, is it?"

"Anyway, Rainbow and George together are two thousand dollars," Mr. Fowler said, not at all worried about Rainbow's feathers anymore.

The woman didn't say anything.

Violet whispered to Henry. "Do you think she'll notice how sad George and Rainbow are?"

Mr. Fowler was impatient now. "If you don't want them, I've got a waiting list of customers. It's not every day you get a macaw and a monkey in a small shop like this. As I said, my boss is coming back. I need to wind up this sale to make room for more animals."

"Very well," the children heard the woman answer. "Here's my check for both."

Jessie felt another elbow poke. This time

it was Arthur. "Can't you stop him? He's not helping tropical animals, he's selling them."

Henry scrambled to his feet. "I'm going to find a pay phone. I'll call Grandfather and Mrs. Tweedy. Mrs. Tweedy might be home by now. Stall them as long as you can."

Jessie led the children to the storage building. They were too late. Mr. Fowler had the woman's check. The woman had the animals and was on her way out the door.

Jessie stepped in front of the woman. "You can't take this monkey or this bird. They don't belong to this shop."

George reached out from his cage and grabbed Violet's jacket. "Yip, yip," he said.

The woman clutched the cages. "Who are you, young lady? And what are you talking about? The manager of this shop just sold these animals to me for two thousand dollars. Now I'll be on my way."

Mr. Fowler hurried over to Jessie and the woman. "What are you doing here?" he asked Jessie. "This is none of your concern."

"But it is *my* concern, Mr. Fowler," a woman's voice said.

Everyone turned around. Mrs. Tweedy stood there, her suitcase at her side, and Grandfather Alden and Henry behind her. "I had the airport taxi drop me here so I could visit all my critters. When I arrived, I ran into Henry Alden and his grandfather, who was passing by. They told me what's been going on."

Mr. Fowler put on a false smile. "All I've been up to is making plenty of money, all for your shop. I got two thousand dollars for this bird and this monkey. You should be pleased."

"I want no part of your side business, Mr. Fowler," said Mrs. Tweedy angrily.

Mrs. Ransome put down the cages and stood in front of Mr. Fowler. "I don't know what this is all about, but it seems awfully fishy. Return my money. Right this minute."

Mr. Fowler fumbled in his pocket. He pulled out the wrinkled check. "Take it."

"And Mr. Fowler, I believe you'll need to speak to the authorities about what's been going on while I've been away," said Mrs. Tweedy. "Please go wait in the shed until they get here."

"You could have a big business here instead of this poky pet shop. And these kids were nothing but trouble. Even mixing up orders and getting guard dogs after them couldn't get rid of them," he said before slamming the door behind him.

"We weren't scared of those big dogs, Mrs. Tweedy, not a bit," Benny said. "And we like this poky pet shop."

Mrs. Tweedy looked tired and upset. "I'm sorry I left you and my animals with Mr. Fowler. I knew he was disorganized, but he turned out to be a criminal, too. As for George and Rainbow, we'll have to find good homes for them."

Grandfather Alden didn't look as upset as everyone else. In fact, he was almost smiling. "You'll be happy to know that I've contacted an old friend about Rainbow and George. Augustus Smith, who is the director of the Habitat Zoo in California, would welcome these two animals."

"Can we visit them someday, Grandfather?" Violet asked.

"Of course," Mr. Alden said, patting Violet's hand.

Mrs. Tweedy was a changed person now that Rainbow and George had a new home lined up. "Let's get these two animals inside the pet shop where it's warm. They can go into bigger cages and stay there until we complete the zoo arrangements. Now I want to hear all about how you found Rainbow and George."

Arthur, who hadn't said anything all this time, spoke up first. "It was me. I was the one who saved, uh . . . George and R-R-Rainbow and Grayfellow, too."

Everyone stared at Arthur. What was he talking about?

"Grayfellow?" Mrs. Tweedy asked, puzzled. "He wasn't missing this weekend, too, was he?"

Arthur nodded his head. "Not this weekend but the other two times. Remember? I saved him once, then tried to save him the second time, but . . ."

Arthur had said too much.

"You said you were looking for your cat," Benny reminded Arthur. "We found Grayfellow and George. Mrs. Doolittle was the one who found Rainbow and called the fire department."

Arthur looked miserable. "I only wanted to help."

Mrs. Tweedy came over to Arthur. She lifted his chin so he could look at her. "Did you let Grayfellow out both times? Just tell me if you did."

Arthur didn't want to look at Mrs. Tweedy, but he couldn't really get away. He looked at the Aldens, too, especially Jessie. "All I wanted was to be a helper in the shop, but nobody asked me. If I saved Grayfellow, I thought you would notice me and let me work here. Grayfellow was my friend, so I took him out. The Aldens almost caught me the other day when I was about to take him out again. I put on my jacket so they wouldn't figure out it was me. I would never hurt Grayfellow. I knew I could always get him back with food."

"Food! Food!" Grayfellow squawked when he heard Arthur.

No one laughed, but they did smile a little.

"So that's why you had sunflower seeds the day you were in the bushes," Benny said. "I have them at my house if you want them back."

Arthur looked at Benny. "Keep them. I don't need bird food anymore."

Mrs. Tweedy put her arm around Arthur. "Of course you do. I want you to help the Aldens once in a while until I get a new manager. You can start today."

Suddenly there was a crash over by the guinea pig cages.

"My goodness, who else is in the shop?" Mrs. Tweedy cried.

There was no answer.

Mrs. Tweedy walked over to the next aisle. "Mrs. Doolittle! What are you doing here at this hour?"

Immediately, Mrs. Doolittle put Doughnut back into his cage. "He was lonely. So are all these other animals on Sundays. You really shouldn't leave them alone so much," she said in her crabby way. "Since you gave me a set of keys and there was no one to visit the animals today, I dropped by."

Suddenly Mrs. Doolittle didn't seem crabby, just lonely.

That gave Benny one of his good ideas. "You should be our helper, too — me and Arthur, Soo Lee and my brother, and my sisters. We have to go to school sometimes, so we can't always come to the pet shop. You could teach me all about the animals."

The Aldens saw Mrs. Doolittle smile at them for the first time. "Well, young fellow, perhaps you don't know that guinea pigs like to rub noses with each other, and with people, too. And that if you're going to train a parrot to talk, you can only teach it one word at a time."

"Can we teach Grayfellow a new word?"

Mrs. Doolittle smiled and stood next to Grayfellow. "What word would you like to teach him, Benny?"

"Benny!" Grayfellow squawked.

"Benny!" Rainbow repeated.

"Benny!" everyone shouted.

GERTRUDE CHANDLER WARNER discovered when she was teaching that many readers who like an exciting story could find no books that were both easy and fun to read. She decided to try to meet this need, and her first book, *The Boxcar Children*, quickly proved she had succeeded.

Miss Warner drew on her own experiences to write the mystery. As a child she spent hours watching trains go by on the tracks opposite her family home. She often dreamed about what it would be like to set up housekeeping in a caboose or freight car — the situation the Alden children find themselves in.

When Miss Warner received requests for more adventures involving Henry, Jessie, Violet, and Benny Alden, she began additional stories. In each, she chose a special setting and introduced unusual or eccentric characters who liked the unpredictable.

While the mystery element is central to each of Miss Warner's books, she never thought of them as strictly juvenile mysteries. She liked to stress the Aldens' independence and resourcefulness and their solid New England devotion to using up and making do. The Aldens go about most of their adventures with as little adult supervision as possible — something else that delights young readers.

Miss Warner lived in Putnam, Connecticut, until her death in 1979. During her lifetime, she received hundreds of letters from girls and boys telling her how much they liked her books.

Let's Have Some *Fur*-ocious Fun!

Here's a mystery only *you* can solve. What has fur, feathers, and puzzles? The answer is: These amazing Boxcar Children activity pages.

The Alden children have gathered together some of their favorite activities and puzzles for you to try. Where does the fun begin? That's no mystery. It starts right here!

Pet Shop Puzzle Pages!

There are some pretty tricky brain teasers on these next few pages. Can you be a pet detective and solve them all? There's only one way to find out: Take out your pencils, markers, and crayons and get ready to solve the puzzles! *(You can find the answers to all of the puzzles in this section on the last two pages of this book.)*

Remember Me?

The Boxcar Children have new jobs. They're going to help take care of Mrs. Tweedy's Pretty Bird Pet Shop! The first thing they will need to do is get to know the animals in the shop.

Color in this pet shop scene. Try to remember everything you see. Then turn the page and circle the correct answers on the memory test.

Remember Me Memory Test

Circle the picture in each row that is exactly the same as the one on the previous page.

Flying Feathers!

Oh, no! Someone has let all the parakeets loose. Can you help Violet and Henry get them back in their cages? Follow the squiggly lines.

Spot the Spots

A customer has brought her identical twin Dalmatians in for grooming. But Mr. Fowler can't figure out which two are the twins. Can you figure out which two Dalmatians are exactly alike?

Clean the Tank

One of Henry's jobs is to clean the fish tank. Can you help him? Take out everything that doesn't belong in a fish tank.

Birds of a Feather Word Search

The Pretty Bird Pet Shop sells all sorts of pets. But Jessie's favorites are the birds. Can you find the names of several types of birds in this word search? The words go up, down, sideways, backwards, and diagonally. Look for **CANARY, COCKATOO, FINCH, LOVEBIRD, MYNA, PARAKEET, PARROT, PIGEON, STARLING**.

```
O D R I B E V O L S
O P A R A K E E T T
T A S N T F G E O A
A Y Y U O R I Q R R
K M C D P E O W R L
C Z B N M H G I A I
O X F I N C H I P N
C V Y R A N A C P G
```

AMAZING ANIMAL CRAFTS!

When the Boxcar Children were living in their little red boxcar, they had very little money. Anything they needed, they had to make for themselves. Even though Henry, Violet, Jessie, and Benny are now living with their grandfather, they still like to make things, only now it's just for fun. Here are two of their favorite craft ideas.

Popsicle Pet Shop Puppets
They are meow-wow!

You will need: Popsicle sticks, pencils, poster board, scissors, markers, glue, yarn.

Here's what you do:
1. Use your pencil to lightly sketch a dog, cat, bunny, or bird on a piece of poster board.
2. Cut the poster board along the pencil lines.
3. Use your markers to draw in the animal's eyes, nose, and mouth.
4. Glue pieces of yarn to the poster board to make fur.
5. Glue a Popsicle stick to the back of each of your puppets to use as a handle.

Make a Puppy Pencil Holder
The pet place for your pencils!

You will need: a small, clean frozen orange juice can with one end open, construction paper, scissors, markers, glue.

Here's what you do:

1. Glue a piece of construction paper to the outside of the can. Make sure you hold the paper until the glue dries.

2. Cut out a circle for the puppy's face. Draw eyes, a nose, and a mouth on the face. Glue the face to the can.

3. Cut out two long puppy ears. Glue one to either side of the puppy's face.

4. Cut out a long construction paper tail. Glue it to the back of the puppy.

5. Use your markers to draw the front and back paws on the bottom of the puppy's body.

6. When all the glue has dried, fill your puppy pencil holder with pencils, pens, markers, and crayons!

Benny's Favorite Jokes!

Nobody likes a good joke better than Benny Alden! Here are some of his favorite animal jokes. They're guaranteed to get you giggling!

What is the best way to ride a pig?
Piggyback, of course!

Why do fish travel in schools?
To show they have a lot of class!

What's the most important part of the horse?
The *mane* part!

Why do chickens scratch?
Because they itch.

Answers
Remember Me:

Flying Feathers:
1D 2C 3A 4E 5B
Spot the Spots:
Two and seven are alike.

Clean the Tank:
The doll, fork, spoon, clock, brush, eyeglasses, and radio should be removed.

Birds of a Feather Word Search:

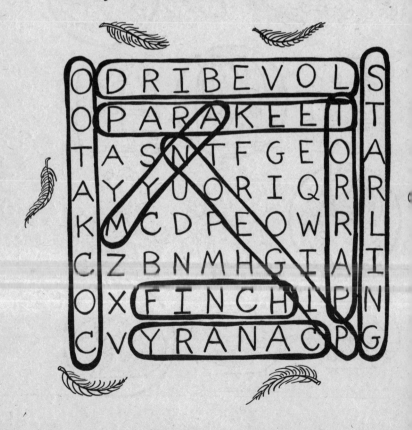